Text copyright © 1986 by Joan Phillips. Illustrations copyright © 1986 by Lynn Munsinger. All rights reserved under International and Pan-American Copyright Conventions. Published in the United States by Random House, Inc., New York, and simultaneously in Canada by Random House of Canada Limited, Toronto.

Grolier Books is a division of Grolier Enterprises, Inc.

Library of Congress Cataloging-in-Publication Data: Phillips, Joan. My new boy. (Step into reading. A Step 1 book) SUMMARY: A little puppy acquires a boy, teaches him some tricks, and finds him when he is lost. 1. Children's stories, American. [1. Dogs–Fiction] I. Munsinger, Lynn, ill. II. Title. III. Series. PZ7.P5376My 1986 [E] 85-30129 ISBN: 0-394-88277-6 (trade); 0-394-98277-0 (lib. bdg.)

MY NEW BOY

by Joan Phillips

illustrated by Lynn Munsinger

A Bright & Early Book
From BEGINNER BOOKS
A Division of Random House, Inc.

Random House 🏠 New York

I am a little black puppy.
I live in a pet store.
Soon I will have
a kid of my own.

Many kids come.

This one pulls my tail.

This one kisses too much.

They are not for me.

Here is another kid.
He says hello.
He pats my head.
Woof! Woof!
This is the boy for me!

My new boy takes me home.

I start taking care
of my boy right away.

I help him eat dinner.

I keep him clean.

I teach him to play
tug of war.

I teach him to throw
a ball to me.

I show my boy tricks.

I sit up.
I roll over.

I teach my boy
to give me a bone
every time I do a trick.

My boy is not good
at everything.

He can not dig very fast.

He can not scratch his
ears with his foot.

He can not hide
under the bed.

My boy can not run
as fast as I can.

I run and run.

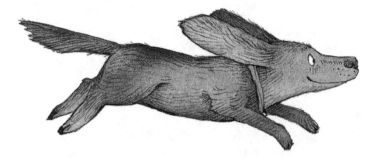

Oh, no!
I do not see my boy.
Is he lost?

I look behind a tree.

I look on the rocks.
I do not see my boy.

Is he on the swing?
No.

Is he on the slide?
No.
I do not see
my boy anywhere.

Now I see my boy.
He sees me too.
He is happy
I found him.

We go home.
Woof! Woof! Woof!
I tell my boy
he must not
get lost again.

My boy is lucky
to have a smart
puppy like me!

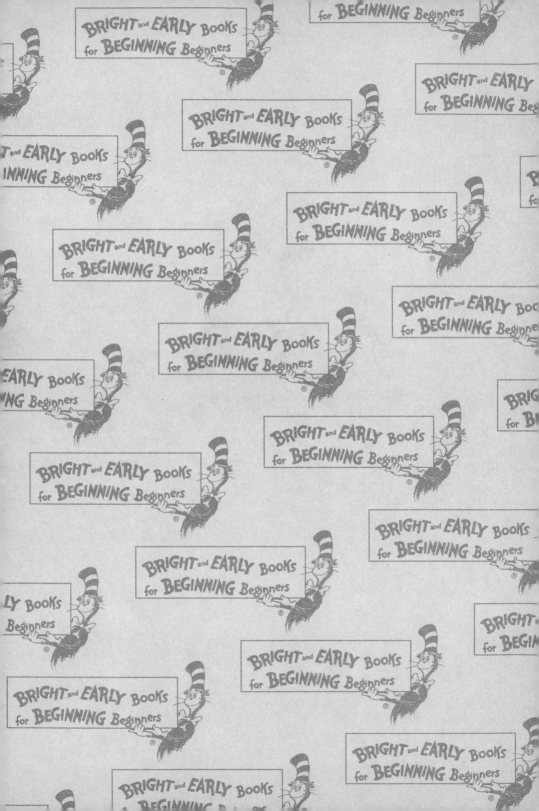